D1060790

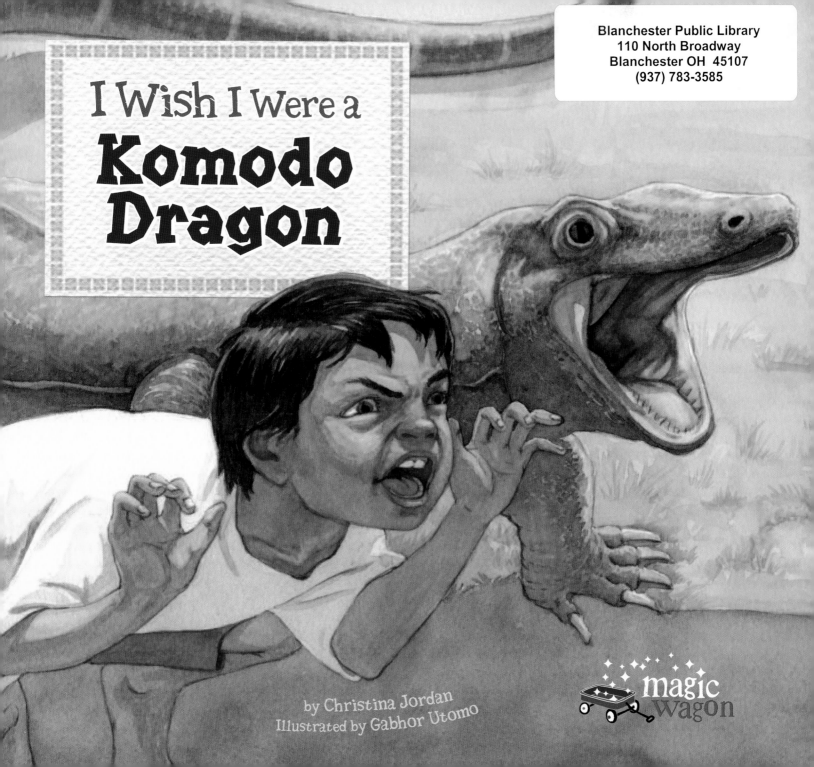

I Wish I Were a
Komodo Dragon

by Christina Jordan
Illustrated by Gabhor Utomo

magic wagon

For my godson, Oscar. — CJ

Published by Magic Wagon, a division of the ABDO Group, 8000 West 78th Street, Edina, Minnesota 55439. Copyright © 2012 by Abdo Consulting Group, Inc. International copyrights reserved in all countries. All rights reserved. No part of this book may be reproduced in any form without written permission from the publisher.

Looking Glass Library™ is a trademark and logo of Magic Wagon.

Printed in the United States of America, North Mankato, Minnesota.
042011
092011
 This book contains at least 10% recycled materials.

Written by Christina Jordan
Illustrations by Gabhor Utomo
Edited by Stephanie Hedlund and Rochelle Baltzer
Cover and interior layout and design by Abbey Fitzgerald

About the Author: Christina Jordan has been an elementary school teacher for 20 years. She also holds a MA in Psychology, is a wife and a mother of three children. Combining her passion for her profession, education, and her family inspired her to add "author" to her list of accomplishments. The "I Wish I Were . . ." books are Ms. Jordan's first series of children's books.

About the Illustrator: Gabhor Utomo was born in Indonesia, studied art in San Francisco, and worked as an illustrator since he graduated in 2003. He has illustrated a number of children's books and has won several awards from local and national art organizations. He spends his spare time running around the house with his wife and twin daughters.

Library of Congress Cataloging-in-Publication Data

Jordan, Christina.
  I wish I were a komodo dragon / by Christina Jordan ; illustrated by Gabhor Utomo.
      p. cm. -- (I wish I were--)
  Summary: A young boy imagines how different his life would be if he were a komodo dragon.
  ISBN 978-1-61641-659-1
  [1. Stories in rhyme. 2. Komodo dragon--Fiction.] I. Utomo, Gabhor, ill. II. Title.
  PZ8.3.J7646Iat 2011
  [E]--dc22   2010048717

I wish I were a Komodo dragon, dangerous and untamed.
My life would be quite different. Nothing would be the same.

The Indonesian islands are the places I'd call home.
Over volcanic rock and rough terrain daily I would roam.

My talents as a ten-foot dragon, they would be quite vast.
I could swim for miles, climb high in trees, and run extremely fast.

8

All these talents would be quite useful when hunting down my prey.
No pigs or birds or any beast would ever get away.

There would be no bullies in my village to mess around with me.
I'd swing my tail (it's five feet long) and those kids would let me be.

With 60 teeth, all razor sharp, I'd be someone to fear.
I'd wander any place I want and no one would come near.

I wouldn't have to share my house with people wall to wall.
I'd live in burrows underground, shared with no one at all.

16

But if I were a Komodo dragon some things might not be fun.
Most of the time I'd be alone, so friends, there would be none.

And if there were no friends for me there would be no one to play.
That means no more games like jacks or marbles after school each day.

19

Curried rice and papaya I could eat no more.
As a mighty Komodo dragon, I'd be a carnivore.

Oh, Komodo dragon, you are so strong and fearsome as can be.
But for now, my life seems cool. I think I'll just stay me.

Fearsome Komodo Dragon Facts

- The Komodo dragon is the largest lizard on Earth. It grows up to ten feet (3 m) long and weighs up to 150 pounds (68 kg).

- When hunting prey, the Komodo dragon hides and waits for something to cross its path. If the dragon's razor-sharp teeth don't kill its prey, its bacteria-filled saliva will.

- The Komodo dragon is an endangered species. That means that it is in danger of no longer existing. People at zoos and other animal institutions work to make sure the Komodo dragon survives for a long time.

Glossary

burrow - an underground home for animals.

carnivore - an animal or a plant that eats meat.

curried - a powdery mixture of spices used in Indian and South Asian dishes.

prey - animals hunted or killed by other animals for food.

volcanic rock - a type of rock that is formed from the cooled lava of a volcano.

Web Sites

To learn more about Komodo dragons, visit ABDO Group online at **www.abdopublishing.com**. Web sites about Komodo dragons are featured on our Book Links page. These links are routinely monitored and updated to provide the most current information available.